GREENE FAMILY SUMMER BASH

PIPER RAYNE

Cover Design: By Hang Le

1st Line Editor: Joy Editing

2nd Line Editor: My Brother's Editor

Proofreader: My Brother's Editor

About Greene Family Summer Bash

Catch up with the Greene family during their annual summer party. There's sure to be surprise announcements and unexpected guests!

a greene family SUMMER BASH

The Greenes

The Greenes

Hank's Kids
Cade Greene (33)
Co-owner Truth or Dare Brewery
Fisher Greene (31)
Sheriff
Xavier Greene (29)
Pro Football Player
Adam Greene (27)
Forest Ranger
Chevelle Greene (26)
Water Boat Tourist

Marla's Kids
Jed Greene (33)
Co-owner of Truth or Dare Brewery
Nikki Greene (30)
Radio Host
Mandi Greene (28)

Owner of SunBay Inn
Posey Greene (24)
Owner of Fringe

<u>**Hank and Marla's Kid**</u>
Rylan Greene (13)

Chapter One

Marla

"HANK, I need more string lights. This isn't enough." I stare up at the pergola and an entire strand that's burned out.

Today's the annual Greene summer bash. Every year, our family hosts a huge barbecue to celebrate the start of summer. We open the pool and enjoy a day with the family, full of laughter and fun.

"I hung two more strands last night," Hank complains.

He's tired from his endless string of jobs when the nice weather hits. People want new decks built, boathouses, pergolas. And my wonderful husband hates to turn people down, so he takes on way too much. Which is why we need this Greene summer bash! Plus it gives everyone a chance to see one another and reconnect as a family. All of our children are busy doing their own things.

Cade and Presley are planning a wedding, Lucy and Adam are still rekindling their love, and Nikki and Logan are preparing for the new baby. Then there's Jed… he's dealing with a complete upheaval to his life. A good one, but it's a drastic change nonetheless. Not to mention, I'm running for mayor of Sunrise Bay, and I'm committed to enough projects myself.

"Please?" I ask sweetly. "You know the kids will stay longer this year, and I love when the lights are lit at dusk."

He chuckles and gets off the couch. "Fine, but I expect payback."

I saunter over to Hank and run my finger down the front of his flannel shirt. "I promise tonight I'll wear that red nightie you like so much."

His hands wrap around my body and he nuzzles his face into my neck, kissing me lightly. "You're crazy. I'll be too tired tonight. But rain check for tomorrow."

I giggle when his teeth latch on to my earlobe. "Done."

"I'll be back." He groans, obviously still not happy to string the lights, but willing because I asked.

He's the best husband anyone could ask for.

As he heads out to the garage to see if we have any left, I go back to the kitchen and pull out the ingredients to make the caramel brownies the kids expect. I used to have so many mouths to feed every day but now that everyone's moved out except Rylan, it can feel lonely. I love when the kids come over and I get to be mom to them.

The garage door opens, accompanied by the sound of a bag landing on the tile floor in the laundry room.

"It was fine. He worked on head goals!" Rylan screams, presumably at Hank. He must've been dropped off by one of his brothers or sisters.

My youngest son walks in wearing his soccer practice uniform, ignoring me and going right to the fridge.

"Hey, Ry guy, how was it?"

"Fine." He grabs the leftover pizza from last night and sits at the breakfast island.

Rylan is different than all his brothers. While Jed

always gave me way too much information on his friends and girlfriends, Rylan is tight-lipped. Cade was already almost out of the house by the time I married Hank, and Fisher and Xavier were right behind him. By the time they felt as though they could trust me, they were grown.

I did have some time with Adam over the years and he always wore his heart on his sleeve—always talking to me and asking for advice. It's amazing how they're all so different.

"Was Calista there?" I try to sound as though I couldn't care less, but I peek up to see his facial expression.

Rylan's cheeks tinge pink and I smile to myself. He and Calista, the girl from the town over, keep getting thrown together for practices by their coach because they're the best in the area. But Rylan's older siblings are always teasing him, so he never opens up about whatever he feels for her.

"Yeah," he answers and bites into his pizza. "I'm gonna go shower."

"You don't want to help me with the brownies?"

He stops with the leftover pizza still in his hand. "Not really. Where's everyone else?"

I huff and wave him off. Rylan has gotten out of doing a lot because he's the youngest. I hope that doesn't bite me in the ass when he grows up.

I finish the brownies and place them in the oven, then I wash the dishes before continuing on with everything else I need to make. Thankfully, Hank suggested we order catering, since the mayoral race is taking so much of my time, so I don't have that much left to prepare.

Heading into the dining room to grab a dish from under the china cabinet, my eyes catch on all the Vote Greene signs. Sometimes I worry I made a mistake, especially with Nikki being pregnant and Jed finding out he's the father of a three-year-old he never knew about. He still needs my help. I should probably toss in the towel on the mayor thing, but it's the first thing I've done for myself in so many years.

I want to prove that I can do more than pack lunches and chaperone field trips and run a small salad dressing company from my house. Not that I didn't enjoy having the opportunity to be with my kids all the time. Some women aren't afforded the opportunity and I've always considered myself blessed that I had the privilege. But deep down, I've always wanted a career. And I grew up in this town. I love this town. I know what's good for this town. Sam Klein is retiring, and I think I have some great ideas that could help Sunrise Bay thrive.

For example, he let the old Grand Hotel sit vacant all these years. Although that's helped Mandi's inn, there are always people who prefer hotels to the homey feel of an inn.

Surely, I've juggled more in my life. I think back to when the kids' father and I split. I've definitely handled more at once. I can be Rylan's mom and a grandmother to Nikki's new baby and Jed's daughter. Leaving the dining room, I feel more confident than ever that I can do this.

Hank's outside hanging the lights, and I spot Cade helping him. Then I hear the laughter of two women in the family room. With a big smile, I follow the noise to see who it is. Our family day is off to a great start.

Chapter Two

Presley

THIS IS my third Greene summer bash and I'm looking forward to it. It's always a great night that no family member is supposed to miss, including the ones who marry in. The Greenes always wrap us up in their warm blanket, reminding us time and time again that we're family.

Cade and I pull in the driveway, Xavier and my sister Clara right behind us. Cade doesn't pull all the way up in case the boys want to play basketball later. After a few beers, there's usually someone egging someone else on, which turns into a night game.

"Hey!" Clara says when she gets out of the fancy SUV Xavier can afford courtesy of his professional football career.

Clara and Xavier are childhood friends who spend a crapload of time together. Lots of the Greenes think they must have a secret friends-with-benefits arrangement because of all the time they spend together, but I'm not so sure.

I hug my sister while Cade shakes his brother's hand,

then we switch and I'm hugging Xavier and Cade's saying hello to Clara.

"Goddamn it!" we hear Hank shout from the backyard.

The boys shake their heads, moving in the direction of his voice.

"Let's go help Marla," I suggest to Clara.

"It's been three years and you don't know yet she doesn't want any help?" Clara laughs.

We stop in the laundry room to grab two Diet Cokes, then when we don't spot Marla in the kitchen, we head into the family room.

"So what's going on with you?" Clara asks, leaning against the back of the couch.

"Other than that I'm gaining weight and pretty soon I won't fit in my wedding dress?"

My mom insisted I go to Boston to get my wedding dress. Even though I just want a small affair here in Sunrise Bay, she said we're not skimping on the dress. I'll admit it, going into the high-end shops in downtown Boston and trying on dress after dress did make me feel like a princess. Clara came with me. Although it was weird at first for my parents to host my sister, whom they didn't know and looks almost identical to me, they've grown to love Clara like I do.

My dress is being made custom for me and I won't have it until a month before the wedding, which means there will be hardly any time for alterations.

"Are you saying you're…" Clara's gaze dips to my belly.

My hand subconsciously flies to my stomach. "No!" I screech. "I've made Cade wear a condom just in case."

She laughs. "Don't you have an IUD?"

I nod. "But Lucy…" That's all I have to say for Clara to nod.

"Good thinking on doubling up the protection."

"I normally wouldn't care if I got pregnant before the wedding—we've been engaged so long as it is—but the dress…" Her eyes glass over. "The dress," she says in the same dreamy tone.

I can't wait to walk down the aisle toward Cade while I'm wearing it. I've envisioned it ever since I shimmied my body into the sample and looked in the mirror. But I've been enjoying way too many cookies and stews and casseroles lately.

"Maybe Logan can help me figure out a fitness plan that will help."

She nods as though that's a possibility, then her eyes light up. "What about Xavier? He's home for another two months before training camp starts. He's already started his running routine."

She's got a point. Logan would teach me to box and get a guy down to the ground. I don't want muscle, I want to shed pounds.

"Doesn't hurt to ask," I say.

"Ask? He'll do it." She waves me off.

Clara's so certain he will—in the same way that a wife or girlfriend is when they volunteer their husband or boyfriend for something. I know Clara and Xavier have been best friends their entire lives, but lately I've been curious about the reality of their relationship, just like the rest of the Greene siblings.

I lean in a little closer to her and drop my voice. "Are you two really just friends?"

She looks quizzically at me. "Yeah. Why?"

Does she really not know what all the other Greenes say behind their backs?

"I'm just curious. You guys are close. *Really* close."

She laughs. "You and I are close too."

"I don't spend every waking hour with you."

If she understands what I'm suggesting, she's not giving anything away. "We've been best friends forever." Clara shrugs.

"But have you guys ever crossed the line? Or have you ever had feelings that are more than friendship for him?"

She shrugs, but a smile tugs at her lips.

"Clara," I persist.

After a long pause, she says, "I'm not blind. I know the man he's grown up to be. He's not the scrawny boy who used to dig for worms with me."

"Do you find him attractive?" I ask, knowing full well I'm pushing buttons.

She sips her Diet Coke and glances outside to where the boys are helping Hank. Currently, it appears that Cade is arguing with Hank about the placement of lights while Xavier is up on the ladder, doing all the work.

"Of course. I mean, he's a quarterback in the NFL. He works out like crazy, easy on the eyes. Plus, he'd do just about anything for me."

"Sounds like there could be wedding bells in your future." My eyes widen as I realize something. "Then we'd have the same last name."

She shakes her head and laughs. I was put up for adoption and have my adoptive parents' last name, while she has our birth parents' last name. Complicated situation.

Then, for some reason, we keep laughing and can't control ourselves. Maybe from the absurdity of what we've been through already.

"Girls!" Marla comes in. "I heard the laughter."

We both sober up and smile. "Hey, Marla," we say in unison in practically the same voice.

"What are you two doing?" She sits down in a chair, so we take a seat on the couch across from her.

We share a look. "Just talking."

She stares at us a moment, a soft smile creasing her lips.

The patio door opens and Cade and Xavier step through.

"Since when did he get so pigheaded?" Cade asks his brother.

"Since you all moved out and he does it all himself," Marla answers.

"Hey, Xavier, Clara has offered to have you train me for a couple months before you leave for training camp."

Xavier looks more like his deceased mother than Hank. He has ash-blond hair, whereas the rest of the Greene boys have their dad's dark locks. His eyebrows shoot up to his hairline and he looks at Clara.

"What exactly did you volunteer me for?" But he isn't upset. Now that I think of it, I rarely see Xavier mad. He's pretty easygoing.

"Pres wants to work out before the wedding, shed a few pounds." She nods toward me.

"I can work her out," Cade says, sliding onto the couch behind me, his fingers running under the hem of my shirt in the back.

"She needs more than just stretching and being limber," Clara says, then looks back at Xavier. "Come on, you know you can work her out good."

"Whoa!" Cade holds up his hand. "Phrase that a helluva lot differently."

Everyone laughs, then we hear the laundry door open.

"Uh huh, they'll have to find another way to get it out. And you can forget going down there and taping the whole thing," Nikki says before she walks in. She stops when she sees us all and Logan hits her back. "What's going on?"

"I think we should ask you the same thing." Marla turns toward her daughter.

"Oh, I'm remaining pregnant forever. If I do my Kegel exercises, I can do it." Nikki flops down next to Clara, her hand falling to her belly that is nowhere near huge yet, and she lets out a long breath. "How did you do this five times?" she asks her mom.

We all laugh, but I think Nikki is serious.

Chapter Three

Nikki

"I GAINED FIVE POUNDS." I stare at my stomach, loving the little human inside but feeling as though my body grows more foreign to me with every day that passes.

"We just came from the monthly doctor visit," Logan informs them before shaking Xavier's hand and going around the room to say his hellos.

"You need to gain weight for the baby," Mom says.

"I know, Mom." When did my voice turn into the sixteen-year-old version of myself? Oh yeah, when I couldn't fit into my clothes and I stopped being able to see my ankles. Not that I want to see how swollen they are already.

"You'll be fine. You have a strong husband who will help you lose the weight after the baby arrives," Cade leans forward and says.

Presley pinches Cade's thigh, and he howls in pain.

What a wuss. I'd like to see him squeeze a baby out of a pinhole.

"Speaking of, why don't you have Logan get you in

shape?" Xavier's looking at Presley and thumbing toward my husband.

"What is he talking about?" I ask the girls.

Clara's busy giving Xavier the evil eye.

"I'm worried I won't fit in my dress," Presley admits.

While I opted for a Vegas wedding—opted might be the wrong word, since I got drunk and ended up having Elvis tie the knot—Presley and Cade are having a big affair in the fall. They've rented out Mandi's inn for all of Presley's family and are getting married on a yacht. I warned them that they could be asking for trouble with people getting seasick, but they didn't care about my opinion.

"You'll be fine," I assure Presley.

I mentally add her concern to the list of reasons why it's good that Logan and I got hitched the way we did—I never had to worry about this stuff.

"What do you want? To lose weight or not have jiggly arms?" Logan asks.

If he was close enough, I'd be pinching him like Presley did with Cade. What is he thinking?

Presley lifts her arms and waves her hand as though she's waiting for her arm to jiggle. "Do I have the bye-bye arms?" Her tone tells me she's about one second from bursting into tears and she's not even the overly emotional one out of the crew.

"No. You're fucking perfect." Cade pulls her closer and narrows his eyes at Logan.

"I just want to lose weight. Running or something," she says.

"I could do some circuit training with you. That way you're building muscle and losing fat at the same time. The more muscle you have, the more calories your body will burn on its own." Logan more than makes up for his remark. "It won't take much."

I smile at him. He better do the same for me when I'm back to only housing one person in my body.

"That sounds great," Presley says.

"I'll join her," Clara chimes in.

I sulk next to them, pissed I can't do the same. Running my hands over my stomach, I allow my head to fall back against the couch. This baby boy never stops moving, which is probably something he gets from his dad. While I'm happy watching reality television at night, Logan has decided that during commercial breaks, he's going to do push-ups and sit-ups. Do you have any idea how pathetic that makes me feel?

Mom pats my knee. "Why are you worried about childbirth?"

"Because someone thought we needed to be prepared." I eye Logan, who sheepishly looks behind him as if someone else is at fault.

"Meaning?" Clara asks, but the twist in her lips says she knows exactly where I'm going with this.

"We watched a birthing tape," I say.

"Oh, Logan," Presley says.

My mom and Clara groan in unison.

"Like the one in health class sophomore year?" Clara asks.

I nod. "More like YouTube. Did you know they have live births on there?" A full-body shiver racks my body as I remember.

"Listen." Logan holds up his hands. "When I was fighting, you saw everything through, learned as much as you could about your opponent, collected all the information you could so you were prepared for anything."

"The baby isn't our opponent," I deadpan.

"No, but you have to be prepared. This way there're no surprises."

I get what my loving husband was trying to do, but seeing a live birth and what's going to happen to my body is unsettling, to put it mildly. We've barely been married that long and now my body is going to change forever. What if… ugh! I shake my head, not wanting to think about Logan never looking at me with the intensity he does now.

"And now how do you feel?" I ask him.

"I'm good. I like to know what we're in for."

I tilt my head. "So you liked the fact that my hoo-ha is going to be ripped open and sewn back together?"

Logan stares for a moment. A noise comes out of Xavier as if he's twelve and just realized how women have babies.

"That doesn't happen to everyone." Mom pats my leg again.

Clara and Presley's faces are now ghost-white. Cade leans in and whispers something to Presley—probably asking if her perfect pussy will be destroyed while delivering his precious baby. And the answer is a resounding YES! Just the thought of a head poking out that hole makes me nauseated again.

"You're going to be fine, and you'll still be the hottest and most beautiful woman I've ever met." Logan sits on the arm of the couch, leaning down to kiss my cheek. "I'm sorry again," he whispers.

Hank comes in from outside. "Lights are up, my darling." Then he notices all of us. "No one thought to join me outside?"

"I tried. You're stubborn," Cade says, which probably means they were bickering. Ever since Cade has tried to step in and act as if Hank is old and unable to do things, Hank works twice as hard to prove him wrong. It's a vicious cycle that drives everyone nuts.

"I hung most of them," Xavier chimes in.

Logan holds up his hands. "Sorry, I just got here."

"How does Rylan get out of helping?" Xavier asks. "We always had to be Dad's helper."

"He just got back from soccer," Mom says as though that's an excuse.

I'm with Xavier. No one had a free pass in our household either. Rylan's the most spoiled kid ever. They better watch out or he's going to be an entitled asshole when he grows up.

"Hey, I hope it's okay, but we invited Gavin Price," I tell Hank and Mom.

"The actor?" Clara asks with piqued interest.

I peek at Xavier from the corner of my eye, and I swear his jaw tics.

"Yeah. He's thinking of buying a house up here and doesn't know many people. Figured I'd invite him to meet our family since we practically make up half the town."

We all laugh.

"It's fine, but just so you know, Grandma Ethel and Dori are bringing Midge," Mom says.

"Someone hide the silverware," Presley says, and we all laugh again.

The garage door opens and shuts, and we listen as someone grabs a drink from the laundry room fridge. Then Posey comes bouncing in looking like she just did five rounds with Logan.

Mom bolts up from the chair. "What the hell?"

Posey waves her off. "Some asshole buzzed by me and my bicycle tires slid off the road and I fell into a ditch. Nothing big."

"You have scrapes everywhere and you're bleeding." Mom is aghast. "What kind of car was it?"

Cade rises off the couch. Xavier steps forward and

Logan stands. Even Hank is leaning closer to hear her answer.

"Some fancy sports car. I don't know. Probably just some tourist." Posey thumbs toward the stairs. "I'm going to clean up. I think you have some of my old clothes around here somewhere."

"I'll be right up," Mom says.

Posey walks toward the stairs and disappears.

The boys all look at one another as though they're deciding who is going to speak first.

"Relax, boys, Posey's a big girl. She can handle herself," I tell them.

They all share a look then sit back down, but no doubt they'll each be looking for a sports car in Sunrise Bay over the next week. Probably even accost a few innocent people in the hopes of protecting their sister.

I shake my head. Men.

Chapter Four

Posey

I'M ALONE in the bathroom for about thirty seconds before there's a soft knock. My mom peeks her head in. I'm staring at my reflection and how bad I look.

"Let me get the first aid kit." She shuts the door as I examine my face.

I tried to play it off when I came in, but seriously—what kind of asshole drives like that? I cannot wait to find him and give him a piece of my mind. Ruining Greene summer bash day sucks, especially since my mom puts so much work into this day every year.

Mom walks back in and shuts the door, but not before Nikki, Clara, and Presley follow her in. They all sit on the edge of the tub like three little humpty-dumpties.

"It's not nearly as bad as you think," Mom says, patting my face with a washcloth.

"What kind of sports car was it?" Nikki asks.

I give her the evil eye because she's just trying for some gossip for her radio show, Scandals of Sunrise Bay. Well, she's not getting any information out of me.

"I'm just concerned for you," Nikki says, but we both know different. There hasn't been a hot story in our small town since her own drunken wedding and we all know she didn't give that story the gusto she usually does.

"We're not putting out a hit list on whoever it was. Maybe it was someone from Northern Lights Retirement Center," I say.

They all laugh because Northern Lights is where my stepgrandma, Ethel, lives with her friends. That should be the focus of Nikki's radio show. They do some crazy shit over there.

"Not in a sports car," Mom says, putting a Band-Aid on my forehead. Great.

"Could you imagine if Dori got behind the wheel of a sports car?" Clara says, and more laughter fills the small bathroom.

I do love my big family, even if they're nosy.

"I'm good, Mom." I step back to stop her from fussing over me. "What can I do to help today?"

She packs everything back up in the first aid kit. "I have everything under control."

I feel relieved she doesn't need help, but even if I didn't feel like it, I'd always put anything aside to help my mom. She did everything for all of us for years before she married Hank and had an actual partner who lent a hand.

"Okay, but let me know if you change your mind."

"Yeah, we can all help," Nikki chimes in.

Of course, she's late to offer. I love my sister, but she can be a tad self-absorbed. Not in a horrible way, but I've always felt as though I was Mom's helper while my other two sisters did whatever they wanted. Maybe it's just because I'm the youngest.

"Let's get downstairs before the boys eat all the food I've prepared," Mom says and opens the door.

I take another good look at myself in the mirror and cringe. Who knew a tumble off a bicycle could do so much damage? I'd be lying if I said I didn't want to kill the bastard who can't control his car. Whoever it is, they're not from Sunrise Bay, that's for sure.

Walking down the stairs, I can already hear the guys laughing and making fun of one another. And Jed isn't even here yet, I don't think.

I'm not surprised when I spot Lucy about to come up the stairs. "Aw… did I miss girl time?"

"Not at all. Posey got run off the road by some crazy guy and Marla was tending to her wounds," Clara tells her.

"What?" Lucy's eyes are wide and filled with concern.

"I'm fine. Look. All bandaged up."

Lucy shakes her head and looks me over to make sure.

"Hey, Luce, thanks for babysitting Bernie," Presley says, and Nikki looks over her shoulder at me and raises her eyebrows.

Bernie is the brother of Lola, Cade and Presley's dog, but the two couldn't be more different. Bernie hasn't grown out of the chewing phase yet and tends to run around in circles, while Lola is chill and lies around the majority of the time.

"You're welcome, no trouble," Lucy says.

"Why did Bernie need a sitter?" Clara nudges her sister's arm, waggling her brows.

"You know Bernie doesn't much care for when we show affection and Cade's been growing impatient. We tried to lock him out of the bedroom, but he whined and scratched on the door, so I couldn't concentrate. I asked Lucy and Adam to watch him as a surprise for Cade."

Mom smiles at her soon-to-be daughter-in-law. "You gotta keep things spicy. I know you're not married yet, but don't let that dog get in the way of bedroom activities."

We all stand in silence in the foyer at the bottom of the staircase. Mom giving us sex advice is uncomfortable at best.

Presley pastes on a convincing smile. "Thanks, Marla."

"Ew, Mom, the last thing I want to know about is you and Hank in the bedroom." Nikki shivers.

"Since I've had to hear and, oh, see pictures of you and Logan, I'd say I know how you feel." Mom crosses her arms and juts out her hip.

"She's not wrong, Nik," I say.

Two months ago, Nikki and Logan got caught by the paps in Vegas while they were there to support one of Logan's friends, who was fighting. They were in the corner of some club and Logan's hand was up Nikki's dress.

"You be pregnant and horny and get back to me." Nikki heads out of the foyer, and we all giggle. For someone who reports gossip for a living, she sure hates when it's about her.

When we rejoin the guys, one thing is clear—Bernie has joined the party. Cade glances at Presley across the room with a look of defeat. Rumor has it he's been through three dog trainers and had no luck at taming the crazy dog.

Bernie spots Presley and runs our way, jumping up, and she catches him.

"Nice, Pres," I say.

She shakes her head. "It was either learn how to catch him or be head-butted over and over. For my body's sake, this is how Bernie and I say hello now."

"I hope you enjoyed yourselves because the playdates are on hiatus for a while." Adam leans back in his chair, a beer in his hand.

"Adam…" Lucy sighs as if they've had a conversation about this already.

Logan's phone rings and he walks away from the group.

"No, I know we were gonna act cool, but that ended when I found him humping Lola this morning. They're siblings." Adam sits up and pets Lola, who's sitting calmly beside his chair. "I'm sorry, little girl. Daddy won't let that happen again."

Bernie gets squirmy in Presley's arms, so she says, "I'm going to take him out."

"Leash is by the garage door," Adam calls.

"I'll go with you," I say, needing to get some air.

Plus, Presley's awesome with advice since she's not from this town and she's marrying in as a Greene. She has a different perspective than the rest of us and tends to be the one we go to.

We walk outside and immediately hear two men's voices.

"Someone else must have arrived," Presley says.

I had been hoping to be able to talk to her alone. I need to discuss these feelings I'm having for someone I barely know but is so far out of my league it's not funny.

Walking out of the garage, I spot the same sports car that ran me off the road parked in the long driveway. Then I spot the guy I've been crushing on. Logan's friend and actor, Gavin Price, stands next to the car that made me careen into a ditch.

"Man, don't tell Cade, but he's one good-looking guy," Presley whispers.

How can I blame her, since he's filled all of my imaginings lately? But instead of the butterflies that usually flutter in my belly when I see Gavin, anger boils the blood in my veins. Because he's the one who almost ran me over.

Chapter Five

Adam

LUCY COMES over to me after Presley takes Bernie, aka Ron Jeremy, outside. Forgive me for not being on the up-and-up of the popular male porn stars of the moment. But Bernie couldn't keep off poor Lola.

"I thought we weren't going to be completely honest about last night, so they didn't feel bad?" Lucy phrases it as a question, but what my wife is really saying is, "I told you not to say anything, so why did you?"

"If the roles were reversed, Cade would be telling us if Lola was lapping at Bernie's dick all night."

"It was not that bad," Lucy says, still whispering as if my family isn't within earshot. They're always within earshot.

"Tell that to poor Lola." I pick her up and cradle her in my arms, kissing the top of her head. "She's probably traumatized. Imagine if I was all up in Chevelle's business." I shudder.

She rolls her eyes. "That's a tad different, don't you think?"

"I think it's the same premise whether it's dogs or humans. Bernie needs to know his place."

"I'm going outside," Cade says and leaves out the back door with Xavier and Clara.

"Can we please put the dog issues to the side today?" my dad asks, then squeezes my shoulder.

Just so we're clear, he's not asking, he's telling in the same way Lucy did.

"You'd feel differently—"

"Adam."

I hold up my hands. "Okay. Okay. Doggie issues are done."

I follow my dad into the kitchen where Marla's cutting up vegetables. After my mom died, there was a long stretch when we didn't have to eat vegetables. It was glorious—until my dad got on this health kick when he finally realized our nutrition was his responsibility.

Lucy sidles up to me as I steal a cucumber and dip it into the ranch dressing. Marla makes her own dressing and it's the best I've ever had.

Marla glances up and back down to the cutting board, but her head flips up again as though she can read that Lucy and I have something we want to say. She most likely can—Marla's a great mom. She always knows when something is up.

"Hank," Marla says, pulling his attention back to the kitchen since he was wandering off. "The kids have something to tell us."

My dad comes back over to the island, then steals a tomato and dips it in the ranch.

She smacks my dad's hand. "If you two keep it up, there won't be any for the guests."

Dad feigns injury. "Why don't you smack Adam's hand?"

"Because I love him more," she says, smiling at Dad.

He shakes his head. "I guess that's the way it should be." Then my dad sets his eyes on Lucy and me. "What's up?"

I look at Lucy to make sure she's ready for this announcement. We wanted to tell our parents first, then sprinkle it out to all the siblings. Wrapping my arm around Lucy's waist, I pull her to my side.

"We've decided to start trying to have a baby," I say. "We've gone back to Dr. Bailey in Lake Starlight, who referred us to a clinic in Anchorage."

Marla smiles and wipes her hands. She's coming over to hug us, I just know it. My dad stays put and stares. After Marla hugs and congratulates us, I look at my dad, waiting for a response.

"Dad?" I've never seen that look in his eye except on the first few anniversaries and birthdays after Mom's death.

"Is this going to put Lucy at any kind of risk?" he asks, looking at me, not her.

"No. I mean, there are risks with anything, but the doctors are encouraging. Lucy will have surgery for her endometriosis, but more than likely we'll be going the in vitro route," I say.

He nods.

"In the meantime, we're going to foster children," Lucy blurts. I was going to wait for that reveal, let them absorb the surgery news first.

"What?" Marla asks, freezing in the preparation of her cucumber and onion salad dressing.

"We've decided that we want to help children who have nowhere safe to go. We'll talk to the fertility doctor, Lucy will have the surgery, and if it's all successful, great. But we still want to help kids who need parents."

My dad steps back and leans against the counter with an expression I don't know how to read.

Lucy moves closer to me. I never thought they'd react like this. I thought they'd be excited for us.

"Aren't you worried?" Marla asks.

My forehead wrinkles. "What do you mean?"

"The heartache that can go along with that. You guys are strong now and a united front, which is wonderful, but that's a lot of balls up in the air."

I look at Lucy and she looks at me. We smile, knowing things might not go our way, but happy we have each other to lean on.

"We understand the odds, but it's something important to us," Lucy says, and I squeeze her into my side.

"Why not just do one or the other?" my dad asks. "Do the in vitro, and if it fails, then look at foster care, or vice versa. Both at once seems like a lot to handle."

I get their reactions now. They're scared because of what happened before when Lucy left me, but they don't have to be. We took over a year to make this decision, so we've thought it through.

"Or we could end up really lucky with our own baby and a foster child," I say.

Marla sets down the whisk, looks at my dad, then back our way. "You do understand that fostering isn't adoption. That the birth parents could get their act together and the child would have to leave your custody."

"We're not fifteen," I say.

"Adam," my dad scolds.

"Sorry. I just mean, we know all the risks and we're not delusional enough to think it's all going to be easy, but it's important to us. Fostering is our way of helping children who may have lost hope. If we can help them, even for the interim while their parents get their shit together, that's worth doing. If we're blessed to be able to adopt them at some point, wonderful. And the fertility thing is something we need to start while Lucy is younger. But we'll be happy and okay as a couple regardless of what happens. We just have a lot of love to give and a home that we'd like to fill with more love."

Lucy raises on her tiptoes and kisses my cheek. "Couldn't have said it better."

Dad nods, and he and Marla share a look. "Sounds like you have it all figured out."

"We do," I assure them both.

"Then congratulations. We wish you luck, and if you need anything, let us know." Marla hugs us both, my dad joining her.

"Pretty soon we're going to have to put an addition on the house," Dad mumbles.

Marla obviously couldn't be happier. Nikki's growing bigger every day, Jed returned home from Minnesota with Emilia, his daughter, last week, and now this.

"We can only hope." Marla smiles at us and winks.

"*Mom!*" Rylan screams and we hear footsteps bang down the stairs. He runs into the kitchen. "Did you invite her?"

Marla looks stunned.

"Hey, Ry guy," I say.

He holds up his hand. "Did you?" He's glaring at Marla.

"What are you talking about?" Marla asks.

"Why is Calista Bailey in our driveway?" He says it like an accusation.

My mouth opens, but Lucy covers it with her hand. Today just got a whole lot more interesting.

Chapter Six

Chevelle

I PARK behind some fancy sports car in my dad and Marla's driveway. I have no idea who it belongs to. My assumption is the guy standing with his back to me, talking to Logan. Probably one of Nikki's podcast guests who knows Logan or something.

Posey and Presley are out in the yard with Bernie, who's pulling the leash so hard, sniffing from bush to bush, it looks as if he's going to pull Presley's arm out of her socket. I grin when I see Posey casually checking out the guy talking to Logan.

I exit my small SUV and I'll admit he's got an ass on him, but he's too thin for my liking. Don't get me wrong, the guy isn't a beanpole, he has lean muscle like a runner, but I prefer guys who bulk up in the gym. The kind who can lift me with ease and put me in whatever position they want.

Just don't tell Hank or my brothers that last bit. They like to think of me as little ol' Chevelle, their innocent younger sister.

A truck roars up the driveway behind me and I don't have to turn around to know exactly who it is. My sixth brother, Cameron Baker. Did you catch that last name? Yeah, it's not Greene, although the man acts like an overbearing big brother and seems to think he's somehow responsible for my safety.

The door of his fancy truck slams shut.

Cameron's family is the richest in Sunrise Bay and he's an only child, which means the fortune and responsibility of the fishing piers will be his one day. Which also means that if I continue running my tourist boating company, I could end up kind of working for him. And that only aggravates me, so I head over to Posey to dodge having to talk to Cam.

"Chevelle, we have something to discuss," Cam says from behind me.

"Later," I say and put up my hand, not even bothering to steal a glance.

The other problem with Cameron Baker, besides him trying to act like my dad? He's exactly the type of guy who gets my lady parts buzzing. He's built, with just enough tattoos to make him sexy but not so much that it covers all his ripped muscles. He's got scruff that I imagine would feel glorious between my thighs, though I try not to think about it. Over the years, he's gone from scrawny to all man. I'm only human, of course I notice.

I've done my own changing over the years, and he's definitely taken notice, but expresses that by ordering me to cover up every inch of my body. Not gonna happen.

Although our attraction to one another is obvious to the two of us, even if we've never talked about it, my brother Fisher is his best friend. Hell, none of my brothers would be keen on Cam stepping over that line with me.

Cam would never do it anyway. Like I said, I'm treated like fragile little ol' Chevelle who needs a fainting couch.

"Hey, girls, who you glaring at? Cam? I know. He's not a Greene, why is he here?" I ask when I reach them, then I notice Posey's Band-Aids and scrapes. "Pose! What happened?"

She touches her face, but her gaze is still glued to the mystery guy.

"BERNIE!" Presley yells and runs after the dog as he takes off.

Cade comes running from behind the house, having heard his wife's shout. That dog is going to have to get his head on straight before Cade ships him off to some doggie military school. I watch the two of them sprint toward downtown Sunrise Bay.

My dad's house is the Greene family home, and it was passed down from my grandma Ethel. It sits high on the hill overlooking downtown, and if you didn't know better, you might think we're fishing out hundred dollar bills from our pockets like the Bakers, but we're not rich. We do all right, all of us work hard for our money, but we don't have Baker money. My grandfather was just good with his hands, wood, and nails.

"Can you believe that asshole ran me off the road?" Posey seethes quietly.

I glance over to see Cam has joined Logan and the other guy whose face I still can't see.

"I think we should put rules in place," I say. "You can't come unless your birth certificate says Greene."

"Or a marriage license," she adds.

"True. So what happened?"

I pull my gaze away from Cam's back. The stretch of his T-shirt—which will soon end up on a lounge chair in the back—over his back muscles sends a rush of heat between my legs. God help me, I need to get laid soon.

"I rode my bike over, but I didn't come from the house. I had to go to Fringe earlier because I promised I'd do Zoe's hair this morning. She's heading to Vegas with Craig for the weekend. Anyway, I'm coming down the road on my bike and that asshole swerved and would've hit me if I hadn't moved out of the way. My tire slipped and I ended up in the ditch. He didn't stop, just kept going. Self-centered asshole."

I love Posey. She's younger than me by two years, which took off the heat of being the youngest after our parents married. My brothers still see me as the messed up little girl who blames herself for causing her mother's death.

I squint when the guy in question shifts his stance so that I can now see his profile. "You know who that is, right?"

"Oh, I do. Gavin fucking Price."

There's something in her tone. Posey's always been free-spirited—even more than me, which is saying something—but she doesn't hold grudges or dislike anyone. She's sweet and kind and good-natured, but I can't help but feel like there's something underlying this hatred.

"The actor. No wonder he drives a car like that. He sure didn't have that ass when he was younger," I say.

Posey scoffs. "It's a rental, and his ass isn't that great."

"So you've looked?" I grin.

"Well, at Mandi's that time I saw it." She shifts in place, clearly uncomfortable.

"But you've never seen it naked?"

She hits me in the arm, her eyes wide. "Chevelle."

Her loud response garners the three guys' attention and Logan waves us over.

"Great. Now I have to be cordial." She walks over there, arms crossed and flicking her long auburn hair over her shoulder.

I roll my eyes at the smirk on Cam's face. The one that says we're going to talk and he doesn't want to hear any objections. He's been on me about this fishing charter I did where I took off my shirt and had on a bikini top. Whatever. I had to put my life vest on, and I'd forgotten to put a T-shirt under my sweatshirt that day. The weather was getting nice… why am I even bothering to explain myself? It's no one's business.

"Gavin, you remember Posey and Chevelle?" Logan says, gesturing to us.

"Yeah, nice to see you again." He tilts his head and takes us in. Gavin still has that charm he had in his younger television days. The charm that made middle and high school girls hang up his picture in their bedrooms.

"You too, but you need to apologize to Posey." I put my hand on her back.

Now that we're face to face with the man, her bravado has vanished. She's staring at him tongue-tied, which I understand. At first, I was tongue-tied when I saw him. I spent most of my adolescent life wanting Gavin Price to be my boyfriend, but now, eh, he's just an asshat who drove my sister off the road.

"I'm sorry." His forehead wrinkles, then he smiles, his dimples indenting his cheeks.

"You ran Posey off the road earlier. See the Band-Aids?" I thumb in the direction of her face.

Gavin shakes his head. "I think I'd remember that."

"Maybe if you weren't fiddling with your radio or whatever. Or had it so loud to begin with, you would have." Posey found her voice. Way to go, girl.

"I promise you, you're mistaken."

She stares at Gavin blankly, and although I want to see her tell him off, I'm more eager to get to the pool and soak up the few months of summer we get around here.

"Don't kill one another. I'm heading to the pool." I strip off my shirt, revealing my bikini top.

Cam's mouth hangs open. "Not in that you're not," he says as though he's my father.

"And I'm going to listen to you why?" I stomp toward the backyard, leaving Posey to tell off Gavin Price now that she's found her voice.

"Because there are guys here who aren't family. Guys who don't look at you like their little sister."

I stop before we reach the patio. Turning, I corner Cam against the side of the house where we're not likely to be seen. "Tell me, Cam, are you one of those guys?"

He laughs and huffs. "Hell no." But he glances down, taking in my erect nipples through the thin fabric of my bikini.

"That's what I thought." I push him out of the way and head to the lounge chair where I plan on remaining the rest of the day.

Chapter Seven

Mandi

COMING to the Greene summer bash isn't something I have time for this year. The inn has been filled every weekend and it's our busiest tourist season. Probably because there have been rumors about Logan Stone and Gavin Price hanging around our small town. Amazing what people will do to spot a celebrity.

Cade and Presley are walking up the driveway when I arrive, so I walk in step with them.

"Bernie ran away again?" I ask Cade, who's gasping for breath.

"If you know anyone who wants a dog." His eyes are pleading as we enter the garage.

"Cade, he's just a puppy. He'll outgrow it." Presley fights for the dog she wanted, but they absolutely got the bad boy of the litter.

I leave them in the garage to argue because we all know Presley will win.

I can already hear Grandma Ethel and her friend Dori in the house when I walk in.

"I'm not sure I see the problem," Dori says. "They train together, why don't they want to be friends?"

They're obviously talking about Rylan and Dori's great-granddaughter, Calista. I feel bad for the kid, because Rylan's at that age where he's intrigued by girls, but they still have cooties. Yet the entire family razzes him about Calista all the damn time.

I'm surprised when I come around the corner of the kitchen and spot Midge with the two elderly ladies.

"Mandi!" Ethel hugs me. "You look beautiful as always."

She's full of it. My red hair is pulled back in a ponytail, and although I have my swimsuit on under my clothes, I haven't decided if I'm going to actually lie out. Glancing out the sliding door, I spot Chevelle in a micro bikini, lying on a lounger. I'm definitely not lying next to her.

I'm pretty secure about my body. Sure, I carry more weight than my sisters, but I don't let it define my existence. I went to college, bought the inn, rehabbed it (with the help of Hank), and I run it successfully. All that and I'm not even thirty yet. I'm comfortable in my skin most of the time. But who wants to hang out in a swimsuit all day when you're not sixteen anymore? Besides Chevelle, I mean.

"Thanks, Grandma," I say.

Ethel isn't really my grandmother. She's Hank's mother, but we all view her as our grandma because she's always treated us like her grandkids.

"You know, I have a grandson," Midge says.

I roll my eyes without her seeing me. "Oh yeah."

"He's about your age. Comes to see me more than my own son. You two should meet up for dinner service at the Northern Lights."

As if a blind date isn't bad enough, let's add glaucoma,

cataracts, and a bunch of gossipy seniors watching us the entire meal. I can imagine it perfectly—a giant spotlight shining down on us while we eat our fruit cups.

"Maybe," I say because I don't say no well. It's a bad habit of mine but one that's earned me close to a five-star rating on the travel apps. I'm a people pleaser and proud of it.

"I'll check in with him," she says. "See when he's coming."

I nod and look at my mom, who gives me a soft smile.

"I'm going outside to get some vitamin D. Nice seeing you all." I give them a small wave and walk outside.

Sure enough, Rylan is in the pool, playing basketball, while Calista sits on the side of the pool, watching. Man, they've grown up.

"Hey, Ry guy. Calista, right?" I smile at her.

"Hi." She gives me a small smile back.

"Mandi, want to play?" Rylan asks.

Usually I'd play with Rylan, because I'd rather be in the water than out, but he has someone he knows here he's currently ignoring.

"I think you have someone else you should ask." I point toward Calista.

She says nothing, but to my surprise, Rylan holds up the ball. "Do you play?"

Calista wastes no time sinking into the water and grabbing the ball. I love that girl and her competitiveness.

"What's up, Chevelle?" I say, laying a towel on the lounge chair next to her. Guess I am going to lie next to her after all.

"I might punch Cam in the face today, but other than that, not much." She shrugs.

Chevelle works outside, so she already has that glow

from being on a boat all day. Me, on the other hand? I'm ghost-white, and my pale skin won't tan anyway. It burns.

"I'm trying to even out my lines." My stepsister points out her short and T-shirt lines. I guess we all have our problems.

I shed my clothes down to my bathing suit and pull out my sunscreen. "Let's go back to the Cam thing."

Cam is Fisher's best friend, and as long as I've been in this blended family, Cam's been around. Hell, he even joins us after Thanksgiving dinner to play games and have dessert, saying that his parents are boring. The guy probably wishes he was a Greene. Right now, he's over by the beer bucket with Adam.

"He's all up in my business." She rolls her eyes. "Love that suit." She touches the fabric because Chevelle does what she wants when she wants. She means no harm in it, it's just her. "Where did you get it?"

I bite my lip, wondering if I should admit it's from a trendy plus-size shop. It's not like it's anywhere she or any of my sisters can shop. I buy the majority of my clothes from the shop even though their fondness for skulls and three-quarter-length sleeves make me a little crazy. It's like they think bigger women don't get cold or something.

"Online," I answer simply.

"Love the cherries," she says. The top portion is white with cherries on it, and the bottoms are just black.

"Thanks."

"Man, I'd kill for your cleavage," she says and looks down at her own chest.

"You'd have to gain the ass to go along with it." I rub sunscreen over my arms and chuckle.

"Fine by me. I'd kill for curves like yours."

She's not saying it to try to be kind. I know she means it. Chevelle means most of what she says.

I decide to change the subject. "Midge wants to set me up with her grandson."

Chevelle laughs. "Be careful, she might kidnap the man to make it happen. Or you."

"Yeah, she'd go from stealing to kidnapping." I laugh, which garners the attention of the guys at the beer bucket.

Chevelle glares at Cam for a moment, then relaxes back into the lounger.

I close my eyes and soak up the sun, kicking summer into gear. It's my favorite season because I'm too busy to think too much about what I don't have in my life—a man. I'm so busy running a successful inn that by the time I get home, I crash in my bed. Okay, maybe I dig into my sex toy drawer, but who could blame me? During the summer, there's not even time for casual sex.

Just as I feel myself dozing off, a girl screams, startling me.

Rylan

CALISTA JUMPS out of the water with a scream and shoots the basketball. She misses the net and I rebound, making the shot. This is so awkward. I mean, we tolerate each other at best and now she's at my house and I have to play host to her.

"I suck," she says before swimming toward the stairs of the pool and sitting down on one.

I don't respond because I'm not gonna be the one who boosts her ego. She doesn't suck, but she's not that good either.

"Do you want to do something else?" I ask.

She glances at me. "I can't believe my great-grandma dragged me here. She told me we were going shopping and would swing by Northern Lights to swim during the family swim time." She crosses her arms.

I try not to notice she has a chest now. At practice, she's always covered up with a baggy jersey. But this swimsuit of hers shows everything. I'm thankful I'm in the water.

"Call your dad to come and get you," I say, because

honestly, I don't want her here. Am I supposed to spend my entire summer bash day entertaining her instead of hanging out with my brothers? They're all leaving and getting married, and I rarely get to see them all at the same time. I was excited to play touch football or Marco Polo or something with them. Now I have to entertain a girl who looks at me as though she wants to kick me in the balls most of the time.

"I'm not gonna do that. Plus, he's working."

"Maybe your mom can pick you up?" I suggest.

She huffs and walks up the pool stairs. "Nice, Rylan."

I roll my eyes and swim away. She grabs her towel and sits down by my sisters on the loungers. I pick up my basketball and keep shooting until Cam cannonballs into the pool and all the girls complain about him splashing them.

I laugh as he steals the ball from me and shoots. Of course, it goes in.

"When Adam was your age, I had to nudge him toward Lucy," he says, never looking my way as he takes another shot. "He was all awkward like you right now and look where he is now."

I balk. He's got to be joking. As if Calista and I would ever end up married one day.

He passes me the ball. "You think I'm joking? Ask them. I made them play chicken and it was love after that."

I shake my head. "Good for them, but as soon as I graduate, I'm out of this town."

Cam raises his eyebrows. "Why?"

"Because I want to play soccer and there's nowhere here to play. I'm gonna get a scholarship, get an education, and hopefully play professionally after I graduate."

I have my entire life figured out, and a wife and kids don't come into my plan until after I retire from playing soccer. The last thing I'd want is to have someone to report to all the damn time.

"You need to live a little." Cam scores again.

Fisher jumps in the pool and takes the ball. "What are we talking about?" He fakes me out and jumps up out of the water to dunk on the net. The flimsy thing wobbles but stays upright.

"Apparently Rylan's got his whole life figured out and it doesn't include the cute girl over there." Cam's gaze lingers where my sisters and Calista sit, but we all know who he's looking at.

Fisher throws the basketball and hits Cam in the head. "Eyes over here."

Cam turns back around and smirks at getting caught stealing looks at Chevelle.

"Don't be one of those people who plan out their entire life. Just live your life and see where it takes you." Fisher passes the ball to Cam while I try to play defense.

"I plan on living my life according to what I want," I say, trying to catch the ball when Fisher throws it to Cam.

Fisher laughs, as does Cam. They think they know everything just because they're older than me.

"When I was your age, I wanted to be a pro football player," Fisher says.

"Definitely not the sheriff!" Cam laughs.

"Fuck no." Fisher abandons the ball and leans back on the concrete ledge, his tattooed arms spread wide. Looking at him now, you'd never think he's the sheriff.

"I wanted out of this town and far away from my family," Cam says, taking a shot on the net.

Fisher points. "Oh yeah, you had big plans for that."

Sometimes I'm jealous of Fisher and Cam and the rest of my brothers. They grew up together, then I came along —most likely a mistake, it was so many years later—so they all think of me as a baby. That I need their advice on everything.

"You're being foolish if you think your life will go according to plan." Cam abandons the game too.

"Give him a break. He's never had anything happen to him that wasn't good," Fisher says.

He's talking about his mom's death. And he's right. I have both my parents and they're happily married. Soccer comes easy to me, and my parents pay to make sure I have a top instructor in the area. I'm sheltered in my big house up on the hill. With so many older siblings, I can pretty much convince one of them at any given time to give me a ride wherever I want to go. Still, it doesn't mean things don't suck sometimes.

"That's true. But he's already swearing off relationships and he's never even had a broken heart."

"And you have?" I ask Cam, because from the reputation he's earned, it seems he's done all the breaking.

"We're not talking about me. We're talking about you. Now get your ass over there and entertain that girl. I know you want to." Cam nods toward Calista.

Fisher stands with a shit-eating grin, waiting to see what I'm gonna do. "You gotta score your first kiss at some point."

I cringe. What is he talking about?

"You don't want it in some lame game with a bunch of witnesses. Trust me." Fisher sighs. "Go make a move."

Some kids at school have gotten their first kiss already. Although Calista annoys me, she's kind of pretty and I like that she loves soccer as much as me.

I toss Cam the basketball and climb out of the pool.

"There you go," Cam yells, and I ignore his jeering.

Calista watches and waits for me to say something

when I reach her. Chevelle and Mandi pretend they aren't eavesdropping.

"Did you want something to eat?" I ask. "Or we could go to the basement and play a video game?"

Calista swings her legs over the chair and stands. She's so close to my height, I cross my fingers I grow taller soon. I'd hate it if she were ever taller than me.

"Do you have Mario Cart?" she asks.

I nod. "Yeah."

"Let's go."

I smile and walk toward the patio doors. She follows until we're downstairs, then she places her towel on the floor. I do the same next to her. A minute later, we're playing Mario Kart alone in my basement and all I can think is that I should've brushed my teeth when I came home from soccer practice.

Xavier

I CATCH sight of my youngest brother, Rylan, leading Calista to the basement. Lucky for him Marla and Dad are outside. Of course, they're more lenient with him than they were with me. When I was younger, Clara and I had to stop having sleepovers at a certain age and had to start leaving the door open. As if I'd do anything with Clara. She's my best friend.

Speaking of which, all the girls, including Clara, are now huddled around lounge chairs in the back, soaking up the sun, drinking margaritas, and gossiping.

"It's like they have nothing else to do," I say, joining my brothers in the pool. Cam throws me the ball and I shoot.

"Well, it's summer bash. We're not supposed to do anything," Fisher says. He rarely gets a day off.

I can't complain. Since I'm in off-season, every day could be like today if I wanted. I spend most of my time working out during the day and my evenings with Clara, either going miniature golfing, where we bet who pays for ice cream, or bingeing the latest Netflix show. We've been doing the same thing every off-season since I got drafted. My life is pretty fucking fantastic.

Cade sinks into the water. "When do you report back?"

"August as usual."

Cade holds up his hands for the ball and Cam throws it to him. "I'm thinking about bringing Presley down to see a game. We need to get away before the wedding."

"About that," I say. Dumbass decided to get married during the fall, which means I have to fly in and out. "I'm flying in on Friday night, and I'm out at the crack of dawn on Sunday. We play on the east coast, so the time difference is killing me."

"Good thing you're not the groom," he says.

"You couldn't do summer?" I ask.

He points at me, then looks at Fisher and Cam and laughs. "Get a load of this guy. Some of us work during tourist season."

"And while you're off, I'm getting my ass reamed on the field."

Speaking of which, I crack my back. It hasn't been the same since I took a hit my last game this season. I'm getting older. Not nearly close to retirement, but the hits, man, they're hurting more and more.

"You also make bank, so I don't wanna hear it," Fisher mumbles.

All of us were quarterbacks in high school, but only I made it pro. Adam might've had the chance, but he found love too young. That was his demise. My brothers support me, don't get me wrong, but I think a small part of them wonders if it could've been them. Not that they don't love their lives, but all they see is the glamour in my job. Not the ice baths, the pain, the media, the pressure of performing. Even during the summers, I worry my workouts aren't enough and if I should be training more.

"I do a lot to earn that money."

"You play, like, sixteen games a year for that money," Cam chimes in, taking the ball from Cade and shooting it.

"Hey now, I played seventeen this year." I grin.

They laugh because they know we made it to one playoff game. The fact I'm the quarterback and most of the pressure rests on me to get us to a playoff game sucks. Especially because I won't even entertain retirement until I have at least one ring on my finger, and I'm not talking about a wedding ring.

Fisher raises his chin at me. "Tell me, what's up with that chick you've been pictured with in the media?"

My gaze diverts to Clara, who either overheard Fisher or is just wondering what we're talking about because she's looking over here. I smile and turn back to my brothers. I don't know why, but I always feel weird discussing other women in front of her.

"She's no one," I say in a low voice.

"The hot blonde with the huge tits? Looks like someone to me," Cam says loudly, and a flip-flop is thrown at his head.

When we all turn around, it's Chevelle who's giving him the evil stare. "Have some respect for women. We're not pieces of meat."

"Stop dressing like a fucking surf and turf meal then." Cam looks at us. "I can't believe you guys don't say anything to her. There's nothing to that bikini."

"Who's here? The only one who would have any interest in her would be Gavin Price." Cade sets his eyes on Cam. "Right?"

The only time I ever see Cam at a loss for words is when it has to do with Chevelle. "Yeah," he croaks.

"And that Gavin guy can't take his eyes off of Posey," Cade says.

"Because he ran her into a ditch," Cam says.

We all stop and stare.

"What?" I ask.

"You didn't hear? He ran her off the road."

"The sports car motherfucker is him?" Cade asks.

Cam nods.

Cade walks toward the stairs and Fisher follows, with me right behind.

Cam puts his hand on Cade's chest. "Relax, Logan dealt with it."

They all look at Logan, who's talking with Gavin at the table and drinking a beer. I'm cool with Logan, and if Gavin is his friend, I appreciate him setting the guy straight. But Fisher tends to be a hothead in regard to family members. He doesn't take them hurting—physically or emotionally—very well, so it's most likely not enough for him that Logan handled it. Pissing off the sheriff isn't a good call for Gavin.

Presley comes to the edge of the pool. "Hey, babe, I'm taking Bernie home. I can't handle this anymore."

Cade gives Cam a look that suggests he'd like to skin him alive for forcing Cade to adopt one of the puppies Cam's dog had.

Cam holds up his hands. "I said no returns."

"Well, tell his mama he's infatuated with his sister," Cade spouts off and walks out of the pool. "I'll go with you."

The two of them head into the house as Cam laughs. Fisher and I look at him.

"Come on, it's fucking funny," Cam says.

While he and Fisher laugh, my gaze travels to the girls on the loungers. Clara is refilling their margarita glasses, and I can't deny the fact she's looking good these days. More confident in her body or something.

I shake my head before dirty thoughts worm their way in. Clara's been my best friend forever and I definitely don't think of her that way. I can just appreciate a nice body. That's all.

"What the hell?" Fisher stares at the side of the house, already pushing off the wall and walking up the stairs toward our unexpected guest.

Fisher

I WALK OUT of the pool and grab one of the towels Marla folded and put in a basket for easy access. I'm not sure what my family would've done if she'd never come into our lives. My dad was doing an okay job after my mom died, but we were struggling for a while. Especially Chevelle.

My grandma and her friend Dori greet the petite brunette walking into the yard. I don't see their friend Midge, which is concerning because she has sticky fingers. Marla might want to check her jewelry box after everyone leaves.

First things first though, I need to figure out what Allie is doing here.

Dori is doing most of the talking, asking Allie if she found the house okay. I don't understand what the hell is going on.

"Grandma. Dori."

Their names are curt off my tongue and my grandma shoots me "the look." The one that suggests she will spank me right here and now in front of anyone even though I'm grown and the sheriff.

"Oh, hey, Fisher," Allie says, waving as if I didn't notice her the minute she came around the corner. Her forehead wrinkles. "What are you doing here?"

"Allie." Her name rolls off my tongue in the same tone as my grandma and Dori's, and Allie's smile dims, making regret fill my chest. "Ethel here is my grandma."

"What?" Allie's eyes widen. "Really?"

Allie's a friend and we hang out sometimes, but I suspect these two grandmas arranged for her to come here so they could try to fix up the two of us.

"You two know each other?" Dori asks.

"Yes," I answer.

"I've known Allie a long time. She helped get my grandson and daughter-in-law together." Dori smiles.

Allie raises her hand. "Guilty as charged. These two are some of the best matchmakers I've ever met."

Allie is pretty much the complete opposite of me. She seems to be happy most of the time, loves gossip and getting in other people's business, and is a nurse. She seems to really enjoy the caretaker role. The differences between us couldn't be clearer.

"I've heard," I say.

Rumors run rampant in both Lake Starlight and Sunrise Bay that my grandma and her best friend are on some mission to fix up every one of their grandchildren. If they think they're gonna fix me up with Allie, they're sorely mistaken.

"We just like people to find love. That's all." Dori smiles sweetly.

"I asked to be on their team," Allie says.

Sounds like something Allie would do. As I said, she's nice and sweet and wants everyone to be happy.

"Can I talk to you?" I ask her.

Allie steps toward me, but Dori steps between us. "Oh, we have plans for Allie."

"Yeah, the summer bash, I assume?" I look around as though Dori is crazy.

"I should say we have someone we want to introduce Allie to." Dori smiles again, but her smile doesn't seem so sweet this time.

I crinkle my forehead. "You're setting her up?"

Dori glances over her shoulder at Allie.

Allie shakes her head as though she has no idea what is going on. "I thought I was helping set up someone else in your family? You guys said I was finally in the fold."

Allie sounds heartbroken that she was brought here under false pretenses. Meanwhile, I'm wondering who the fuck they're setting her up with and why the hell it's not me.

"Don't worry, sweetie, your time will come." Grandma pats my arm.

I narrow my eyes. "What? I don't wanna be fixed up."

"You have that look on your face, like you did back in high school when—"

She finally gets the hint to be quiet when I glare at her. I know what she's talking about and I do not look like that right now.

"Hey, ladies, I totally appreciate the setup," Allie cuts in. "I mean, you ladies know your stuff. Nine successful matches with Dori's grandkids, but—"

"Technically we're at thirteen between the families. Marla and Hank, then my three grandchildren, Cade, Adam, and Nikki," Grandma Ethel corrects her.

I groan.

"Well, regardless of the number, I'm not really into being fixed up right now. I want to do the fixing up."

Dori links arms with Allie and points toward the pool. I glance over my shoulder to see Cam coming out of the water.

"That's Cameron Baker. He's sweet like you and so personable. Gets along with everyone. He's funny and his family owns the fishing piers." Dori whispers the last part.

"He's good-looking. Look at those thighs of steel," Grandma Ethel says.

I cough up bile from my grandma remarking on my best friend's thighs. What the hell?

"He looks nice and all, but I'm just not interested in a relationship at this point," Allie says nicely as though she's trying to let them down easy.

Grandma Ethel slides her arm through Allie's other one so that the two of them have her locked into place. "One date. Sparks might fly."

Cam stands over Chevelle and shakes his hair, spraying droplets of water all over her.

"Jesus, Cam!" she screeches.

"Oh sorry, didn't see you there." He laughs and walks away. So immature.

Chevelle stands and pushes him back into the pool on his way to get a towel.

He springs from the water. "Want to join me?" He winks at her.

I hate the way he tows that line between flirting and joking around when it comes to my little sister.

"In your dreams," Chevelle says and sits back down in her way too small of a bikini. But I've learned there's no point in saying anything because she'll just dig her heels in harder.

Both grandmas watch, fascinated, as if they haven't seen Cam and Chevelle fight all their lives.

"I'm starving. Can I eat something first?" Allie asks.

"Sure, I'll show you where everything is at." I twist around to let her walk in front of me.

Somehow, she escapes the grandmas who are now whispering to one another.

"I'm sorry," I say.

Allie shrugs. "I know how those two work. I've known them for a few years. I'm such an amateur though. I should've realized why they asked me to come today. It wasn't to help them."

I hand her a plate, and while she's filling it, I spot Jed walking into the backyard with his daughter, Emilia, in his arms. She's asleep with her head on his shoulder. None of us have gotten a ton of time with her since she's only been in town for a week and we're trying not to overwhelm her.

"Is that Jed? With his daughter?" Allie whispers.

"Yeah." It's still surreal that he has a three-year-old daughter he never knew about.

"Man, there's something about a man with a child in his arms that makes your ovaries explode." I stare at her and she eats a carrot dipped in ranch. "What? It's true. I realize you don't understand it because the same thing doesn't happen to you when you see a woman with a baby."

"What does that mean?" I ask.

She shoots me a look. "You're a man. Very different thinking when it comes to these things."

We watch Marla take Emilia from Jed's arms. One thing I've noticed is that he's letting his mom do too much of the caregiving. He's gonna have to man up soon because he's all that little girl has—with the exception of all her aunts and uncles.

"I can see the appeal of a single dad now." Allie hasn't taken her eyes off Jed. Although I shouldn't give a shit, something inside me wants to roar to life.

I leave Allie at the table to get a hold of myself, and Rylan walks past me, grumbling. "Why do they have to keep poking into my life? As if I want to spend the after-noon with Calista Bailey."

I can't disagree with him. At some point, things are going to go south with Ethel and Dori's matchmaking plans.

Chapter Eleven

Lucy

WATCHING Marla gracefully remove Emilia from Jed's arms, I catch Adam's lingering gaze. We both hope to have that one day. And I'm almost certain we will, whether it's in the form of adoption or one of our own.

I follow Marla with Emilia up to the room she plans to decorate for her new granddaughter.

Jed's still outside and already has a beer in his hand. We all know this hasn't been the easiest of transitions for him, but I know he'll turn it around. He's way too good of a person, plus I see his love for Emilia. I think he's just worried he won't be a good enough parent. I think it's the caring part he feels he's not capable of. Which is why Marla is the one taking Emilia upstairs.

"Hey," I whisper.

Marla's struggling to get Emilia's coat off without waking her. I sit down and help Marla get Emilia's arms out of the jacket. I'm not sure why she's wearing one when it's a beautiful summer day, but I would never question Jed about it.

"Mommy," she says in a soft voice.

Both of us freeze, looking at the other.

"Go to sleep, baby," Marla whispers and lays the little girl on the twin mattress that used to be Jed's when he lived here briefly before college.

I look around the room. There are still pieces of the glorified prom king Jed once was present in the room. There's a picture on the dresser of the double dimple smile that won over every girl in the school. But Jed swore off any kind of commitment early on. Never interested. Now he's got this angelic girl to raise.

Once Emilia is settled, I walk out of the room. Marla's right behind me, turning on the intercom and shutting the door. She went out and bought everything when we got the news about Jed bringing Emilia home after the paternity test results revealed that he was the father.

Just like with any other tough time this family has had, the Greenes all got together, redoing Cade's old bedroom in the boys' house to be suitable for a little girl. Now only Jed, Fisher, and Emilia live there.

"It breaks my heart," Marla says, shaking her head.

We walk down the stairs. I'm not sure what to say because I don't know if she's referring to Emilia growing up without a mom or Jed's lack of parenting thus far.

So I just nod in agreement because I feel for the girl on both accounts. Although I know in my bones that Jed will stand up and be the father he needs to be. He only needs some time to adjust to his new role.

Marla stops in the kitchen. For a moment, I watch her staring out the window to the backyard. Although I have a mother of my own and we rekindled our relationship after my accident, there's still a pull inside me to watch over Marla like any daughter would her mother. I see the worried lines on her face.

Instead of joining the others, I go over to the sink and grab a dish towel to dry the dishes Marla's pretending to clean when really, she just needs time.

"You know he'll be okay, right?" I say in a soft voice. "He'll come out of this fog and be the dad he needs to be."

She glances over and nods. Jed's still got a beer in his hand and he's sitting on a chair with his phone in his hand. "I hope so, but there's a lot about Jed he doesn't like others to see. Scars that he hides well."

Since Adam and I are so much younger, Jed was long gone when we entered high school, but Adam's told me enough that I understand what she's saying. Jed fights his own demons when it comes to his dad.

"I know, but he's too kindhearted and protective of the ones he loves to do anything other than be the father Emilia needs."

She turns to me, stopping the washing, and there are tears in her eyes.

"Oh, Marla," I say and open my arms to hug her. She's done so much for me over the years, this is the least I can do. I want to smack Jed over the head and tell him to shape up, like a basic training drill sergeant.

"I'm fine. I really am." But her voice trembles.

The back door opens and Hank stops, a dish in his hands, watching us for a moment. Then he puts the serving tray on the counter and nods to me that he'll take over. Soon Marla is in his arms, her head buried in his chest.

"Go enjoy the party, Luce," Hank says.

I do without looking back, because I know Hank can make Marla feel better. Adam is so similar to his father in the way that they care for their family.

When I step outside, Adam's in the water and the girls are gossiping about some new reality show they're all watching. I sit on the edge of the pool and dip my feet in.

"I'm out," Adam tells his brothers, tossing the basketball at them. His eyes remain on mine, clearly sensing some shift in my mood.

Sometimes I can't believe I was lucky enough to win him twice. "You don't have to quit on account of me."

His palms skate up my inner thighs, parting them so he can slide between. "You always come first."

I smile and push my fingers through his wet dark hair. We stay there, not exchanging a word, though I hear his thoughts as my own. Will we get through these coming months of fostering and me going through all these medical procedures? It's a lot to take on, but we took the year to really figure out what we wanted and now we need to hit the ground running. It might not be easy, but at least it's summer break now, so I'm off from school.

He rests his chin on my thigh and looks up at me. "You okay?"

I nod. "I'm perfect."

He gives me his best smile, but it doesn't quite reach his eyes.

"Adam, relax. We're together and we're going to get through this. Hopefully with a child."

He places his hands on the edge of the pool and uses his strength to push himself up and kiss me on the lips. "With at least one child." Then he falls back into the water.

"At least one?" I raise an eyebrow.

He smiles wickedly. "Maybe a dozen."

I put my foot on his shoulder and push him away. He pretends to sink but pops back up.

"We could only be so lucky." I sink into the water and he grabs me by my waist.

"Just like old times. Want to play chicken?" he whispers, keeping us away from everyone else. Memories of his twelfth birthday resurface in my mind.

"You should've kissed me," I joke.

"Kissed you? I was twelve. I didn't understand all the shit happening with my body. You ruined me at twelve."

I hug him. "Does it help that you ruined me too?"

His chest vibrates with laughter. "Definitely. I love you, Luce," he says.

"I love you, Adam."

"Jed, I need to talk to you," Hank says so loudly everyone stops talking.

All eyes focus on Jed sitting at a table of six all by himself, nursing a beer. He raises his eyebrows but stands and tucks his phone in his pocket, following Hank around the side of the house. All the Greene siblings look at one another because it's not like Hank to hand out a fatherly lecture during a party. But then again, he just consoled his wife, and everyone knows that like all the Greene men, Hank's wife takes top billing now that all the kids besides Rylan are grown up.

Chapter Twelve

Allie

"YOU'RE ALLIE, RIGHT?" Cameron Baker asks when he approaches me at the table.

Although Cameron is Fisher's best friend, we've never officially met. Mostly because I usually only hang with Fisher after we're both off shift for a night. He comes into the hospital for some accident or case he's working, then we grab a drink at quitting time. We've been to the gym together a couple times but we're not gym buddies. But I've heard enough stories about Cameron to know he's not the guy for me.

"That's me."

He sits in the chair next to me, snatching a deviled egg from the food that's sitting out. "I'm Cam, Fisher's best friend." He swallows the egg in only two bites.

"I know who you are." I move the pasta salad around my plate with a fork.

"Does my reputation precede me?"

I raise both eyebrows. No way this guy is as arrogant as

he seems. Fisher would never hang out with someone like that. "Fisher. He's told me stories."

He cringes. "That can't be good."

I continue to eat, not really entertaining the conversation. Mostly because I'm upset at myself. I wanted to fix someone up. I had no idea Ethel was Fisher's grandma. I didn't even know her last name—which seems weird now that I think about it. And it wasn't like when she gave me directions to this place. She told me it was the Greene family home. Still, I was so excited for today. All to come here and find out they want to set *me* up. Likely with this guy and his pretty bad boy frat guy persona. Cam's hard to explain. Not nearly as inked as Fisher, but enough to not seem preppy, but then his family money and his arrogance paint him as a frat boy.

Fisher joins us, bringing over three beers, and sits on my other side. "Cam, you met Allie?"

"I did. I see why you've been hiding her." Cam pops open his beer bottle.

"Ew," I say.

Fisher shoots him a warning glare. "That's not what's happening and cut it with the bullshit."

"It's just a line. Relax. Sorry if I offended you." Cam looks at me, and I can't tell if he's genuine or not. "It was meant to be funny. Everyone is tense since Hank called Jed away." He grabs another deviled egg and pops it in his mouth.

"I'm sorry, I'm just bummed." I fork my salad and put a bite in my mouth.

"Why?" Cam asks, muffled as he's still chewing.

I eye Ethel and Dori across the pool talking with Marla, Fisher's mom. I met her in the hospital once. Midge sits off to the side under the shade of a lounger. I think she's napping.

"Thelma and Louise? What did they do?" Cam snags a chip from the bowl and pops it in his mouth.

"Why don't you just make yourself a plate?" I ask.

"Because Cam doesn't like to be tied down. Not even to his own plate at a family barbecue." Fisher takes a pull of his beer.

Damn, he looks good in just his bathing suit. Not that I didn't think he wouldn't. I'm not sure which I prefer, Fisher half naked or Fisher in his sheriff uniform. I've been to the gym with him a few times and Fisher in his workout gear is pretty great too. They're all core-clenching.

Cam picks up a chip and throws it at Fisher. "Shut up, man, you make me sound like a manwhore."

Fisher says nothing but raises his eyebrows, and Cam throws another chip at him.

"It's not about the women, it's about the freedom." Cam's attention is centered on me now. "No offense."

"Why would I take offense?" I ask.

"Because I was the guy they wanted to fix you up with, right?"

Man, news travels fast around this family.

"You or Jed, I think," I answer.

"Jed's your better bet. He needs a baby mama," Cam says.

Surprisingly, Fisher says nothing. For some reason, I'm disappointed.

Just then, a gorgeous brunette walks into the yard from the side of the house. She's in a bikini top and denim shorts with a bag slung over her shoulder. She looks familiar, but I can't place her.

"*Mol!*" Fisher's stepsister, Nikki, screams. "About time. What happened to the solidarity of a one-piece?" Her voice turns sinister, and everyone laughs.

"Molly not show off her body at a pool party? What

planet is Nikki from?" Cam stands. "It was great meeting you. Let me know if you need me since Fisher here isn't one to fill a conversation with words."

"Fuck you," Fisher mumbles.

Cam walks away and gravitates toward all the Greene women.

"So you're that disappointed about the fixing up thing?" Fisher asks without actually looking at me.

I lean back in the chair. "You have no idea. When I helped them with Kingston and Stella, they acted like I could be a part of the team, then they disappeared on me. I mean, Kingston's sister Sedona rekindling her relationship with an old flame wasn't exactly hard work. The two of them had sexual tension for miles. Plus, they had Palmer."

"You know the Baileys well?"

I look over at him and his forehead is creased.

"Stella is a friend. I worked with her when she first came back to Alaska, and I've been invited to some family parties. I don't know all of them, but I know *of* them if that makes sense. Unlike your family. You should feel ashamed that you haven't introduced me to them."

I eye him hard, although I'm not mad. Heaven knows I wouldn't bring Fisher around my family right now.

"Believe me, you should be happy I kept you out of the chaos," he says and slides to the edge of his seat. "I can do some quick names and who they are, but you'll never remember."

"Ha! I am so good with names, you'd be amazed. Plus, I've always wanted to be part of a big family. It must be great."

Fisher stares at me for a beat too long, as if I'm crazy. But I shrug. Who wouldn't want to have all this all the time?

After he points out his sister, brothers, stepbrothers, and stepsisters, as well as some of their significant others, he stands. "Now that that's done, want to go for a swim?"

Looking at Fisher's ripped body, images come to mind that shouldn't. So I strip off my T-shirt because maybe if his annoyingly gorgeous body is underwater, I'll stop thinking dirty thoughts. But his gaze falls down my body, and a shiver runs up my spine.

Crap, I think I made a bad decision.

Chapter Thirteen

Cade

LEAVING my entire family out back, I round the side of the house and find Jed and my dad talking while shooting baskets on the driveway.

"All I'm saying is I understand how lost you feel, but imagine Emilia. Think about her." My dad shoots the ball.

"Fathers usually have nine months to figure this shit out. I had a couple weeks to prepare to have a kid. Hank, I'm not the 'number one dad' T-shirt-wearing kinda guy."

"Then be the 'number one dad' mug kinda guy," my dad says.

Jed blows out a breath, shoots the basketball—missing his shot by five feet—and spots me from the corner of his eye. "Am I being ambushed?"

I grab the basketball and dribble around.

"You're not being ambushed," I say, shooting and scoring.

My dad grabs the ball.

Jed puts his hands on his hips, his head falling forward in defeat. "I'm gonna fuck her up."

"You're not gonna fuck her up," I say.

He peeks up through his long eyelashes. The ones women go crazy over. The same ones Emilia has. "My dad fucked me up. Fucked us all up."

I throw him the ball and he catches it. "Sure, but we straightened your sorry ass out."

Jed chuckles, but I know we're far from making progress.

Hank sighs. "Having your mother do all the parenting on your behalf isn't going to make it any easier on you."

Jed shoots and misses again. "I can't even make a fucking basket."

"You're being way too hard on yourself." My dad grabs the rebound and shoots it. "When Laurie died, I wasn't the best dad I could be. I sulked, and when I was done sulking, I was yelling because I was so pissed at what the world did to me."

"How could her mother name me on the birth certificate and never tell me? If she'd lived, I never would've known my daughter."

And there's another reason Jed's struggling so much.

"I'm so pissed at her mother, but at the same time, Emilia's suffering from the loss." Jed squats and runs his hand through his hair. "I'm so fucking lost I have no clue what to do."

I put the basketball down and sit on the concrete driveway with him.

My dad joins us a minute later. "It's not gonna be easy, Jed. But you have to put down your walls. Kids don't understand walls. They don't understand guilt trips and grudges."

Jed doesn't bother looking up. Not out of disrespect for my dad, but growing up, Jed didn't have the best role model. His father praised him, bought him whatever he wanted. During senior year, that meant buying off the coach so Jed could be quarterback. Screwed me over, but that's under the rug now. I only see Jed as my brother and best friend. But his dad was just empty promises because under it all, he was selfish and did whatever he wanted at the expense of his family.

I say, "I know you didn't plan on having kids right now. That you might—"

He picks up his head and looks me square in the eye. "I never planned on having kids—ever. I'm not like you, Cade. I don't want a wife or a kid or any of that shit."

His words pierce me like the tip of a blade. How did I never know that?

"You're letting your pain from the past speak for your future." My dad puts a hand on Jed's shoulder.

Jed shrugs it off and stands. "This has nothing to do with my dad. I couldn't give a shit about him. Thanks for the talk, boys, but I got this handled all by myself."

He stalks away, and my dad looks at me once Jed's rounded the house. "I swear to God, I'm not raising another kid. Once Rylan's out of the house, we're done."

My dad stands and disappears into the backyard. I stand and brush off my ass. I know Dad doesn't mean it in a mean way, but he's spent the majority of his life raising kids. Starting over if Jed doesn't take on his responsibility is a possibility, because there's no way Marla would let go of her granddaughter. Nor should she. The only solution is for Jed to step the fuck up.

"Hey, you." Presley comes around the corner. "Your dad's face is all red and he looks mad."

She slides her arms around my waist, and I pull her to me, kissing her forehead. "He's mad at Jed."

How could Jed not want this? This feeling of having someone in your arms that you love so much you can't breathe at the thought of losing them? I get his problem. I had to overcome some shit because of my mom dying and not wanting to put my heart out there, but the reward is worth it. I tighten my hold on Presley and she snuggles her face into my neck. I'd be lost without this woman.

"Hey, babe?" she says.

"Yeah?"

"I can't breathe."

I release my arms. "Sorry."

She looks at me with that expression like I'm in charge of all her happiness. Talk about putting a giant S on my chest and making me feel like I could fly. "Don't be sorry, I like it when you hold me tight. Makes me know you don't want me to leave."

"Never. I never want you to leave."

"Well, I don't plan on going anywhere."

We smile, and I place a chaste kiss on her lips. How did I ever get so lucky?

"Come and swim with me." I take her hand and lead her to the back of the house.

I spot Marla now holding Emilia in her arms in the rocking swing. She must not have been down long for her nap but she still looks tired. She's plastered to Marla like a koala bear, and Marla's eyes are closed with her lips right by the little girl's ear.

I shake my head. "Jed better get his head out of his ass and soon."

"Maybe all he needs is the right woman to make him see the possibilities."

I glare at my fiancée. "The last thing he needs is a woman."

She shrugs. "The right woman worked to get your head out of your ass."

Presley smiles and runs off, but I catch her, lifting her and jumping into the pool.

She's right, but I'm not telling her that.

Chapter Fourteen

Jed

FUCK my family and fuck all this shit.

I sit my ass on the front step of my mom and Hank's house. All the noise from the party out back echoes in the air around me. I'm surprised Emilia can even sleep. Then again, she must be completely zonked out since she rarely sleeps through the night.

I used to spend my nights playing video games, heading to a bar to grab a drink with friends, or just generally doing whatever the fuck I wanted. Now I'm tiptoeing around the house, washing tiny clothes, and trying to soothe a girl who looks at me as though I'm the goddamn IT clown. The only thing I have going for me is that I'm a killer chef for a three-year-old girl's palate. Mac and cheese, chicken tenders, tater tots—she loves what I feed her. That's the only part I'm winning so far.

Does Hank think I *want* to hand over my daughter to my mom?

Hell no, that's not me.

But Emilia sees something in me and I'm pretty sure

it's fear. Which does neither of us any good. She's scared because her mom died and she's been left with a stranger, and I'm terrified because I cannot screw her up. Not the way my dad did with my sisters and me.

The knife to the heart is when Emilia laughs at Fisher. Since Adam and Cade both moved out, it's only us in the old Greene house now. Fisher tickles her, and she laughs. He turns her into a flying airplane, and she laughs. The guy eases the tension well enough, but I swear I think he's better suited than me to be her father.

"What are you doing?" Bibi—which is what I call Ethel, my stepgrandmother—comes around the house. "I wondered where you were."

"If you're here to lecture me, your son beat you to it," I grumble and pick up a weed growing through the mulch.

"I don't lecture. You have two other grandmas, you don't need a third."

I cock my eyebrow at her because I consider her my grandma even if it's not by blood. And from what I know, she likes that.

"Okay, so why aren't you enjoying the party?" I help Bibi to sit next to me.

"To tell you a story. When Hank was first born, my husband was so afraid. You know the soft spot on a baby's head and how they're so tiny? He thought for sure he was going to hurt him. He'd say, 'Ethel, my calloused hands will scratch him.'"

I tear the weed into pieces, unsure why she's telling me this. I mean, I get where she's going with it. My entire family is trying to push me in the right direction. And it's not like I'm going to abandon my kid or something, but Jesus, give me a moment to catch my breath.

"I faked sick for an entire week. Pretended I couldn't get out of bed." She chuckles. "He had to cancel all his appointments and take care of Hank for an entire week with no help from me."

"That's kind of evil."

She nudges me with her shoulder. "Nah. After that week, he'd come home and swoop Hank right up into his arms. It's what women who love you will do. Show you how to be the best version of yourself you can be." She winks.

"Well, I don't have a woman, nor do I plan on getting a woman."

Her shoulders fall and she stares at the side of my face because I refuse to face her. "Jed Greene, do not tell me you're one of those bachelors who thinks he's going to be scoring with women half his age when he's old and gray?"

Hell no. I'm not my father. Still, there's no way I'm about to go into all my issues with Bibi right now.

I say, "I'm sure as hell not getting married."

"You have that charm." Her tone is so matter-of-fact it catches me off guard. "You could probably have any woman you want."

"I'm not sure about that." Tanya Eaton, aka baby mama, clearly didn't think I had what it takes to be a father. Hence the reason she never bothered to tell me she was pregnant.

Grandma Ethel knocks her shoulder to mine again. "You do. All the women down at Northern Lights love you. Always asking about Jed. So easy on the eyes. It's because you compliment them all the time." She nods.

My charisma was inherited from Jeff Greene, my dipshit father. It gets me in trouble. Always has. The other thing that gets me in trouble is my wandering eye. The one that suggests no woman will ever be enough for me, which is why I never wanted kids. I never want to do what my dad did to us.

I shake my head to get rid of the thoughts. "Bibi, I'm friendly. That's all."

"You should go out back and talk to Allie."

I crinkle my brow. "Allie? As in Fisher's Allie?"

"No, she's my Allie. Actually, Dori's I suppose, since we were fixing up Kingston when we met her." She looks about as confused as I am.

"The only Allie I know, and the one who's at this party, is Fisher's friend."

Her gray eyebrows scrunch together, and I see her wheels turning. If I'm lucky, they'll turn right around to fixing up Fisher and Allie and she'll get off my back.

"Huh," Bibi says. "Regardless, do you really want that sweet little girl to grow up without a mommy figure?"

I bury my head in my hands, massaging my temples with my fingers. "Fucking hell. I love you, Bibi, but I can't have this conversation right now."

I walk away from her, rounding the side of the house, and find Molly headed in my direction.

"Hey, you," Molly says. "I was just trying to find you."

Molly's wearing the skimpiest bikini she could get away with at a family event, and even in my shit mood, I notice.

"Hi."

"Emilia is fast asleep in your mom's arms," she tells me.

But all I want to do is forget about all this for a little while. Forget that my life's been flipped upside down so fast my head is spinning.

And Molly's tits look mouthwatering in her bikini. You'd think she put ice cubes on her nipples the way they're pointing through the fabric, begging to be sucked.

I glance around to make sure no one is around, then I take Molly's hand and guide her back toward the front of the house.

Chapter Fifteen

Molly

JED'S HAND slides in mine and he leads me to the front of the house. We watch Ethel's back as she goes the other way around the house, then Jed opens the front door, sliding us into his family home.

Nikki would kill me if she knew I've been fooling around with her brother. It's not like this is anything serious between us. It's two grown adults having fun together. Pure lust and pleasure. It wasn't my plan to come here today and entice him, but I see the stress he's under. I just want the happy Jed to come back. No harm, no foul, right?

"Come on," he whispers and guides me up the stairs to what I think was Posey's bedroom once upon a time.

Quietly, he shuts the door. The voices from the party drift up to the second floor, but it's as though Jed doesn't hear them because his hands land on my face and his lips on mine in seconds. His tongue dives into my mouth and I meet his eagerness with a ferocity of my own.

"You're killing me in this thing," he says, his fingers

making quick work of my bikini top. Then his hands are on my breasts, massaging, twisting, teasing my nipples. "You did it on purpose. Just to turn me on."

"No," I lie, because of course I did. I feel as though I've been dressing for him for most of my life. It's pathetic, I'm aware.

"Liar. It only makes me want you more."

"Then yes, I did."

His hands grow firmer, tightening on my breasts. The feeling of him touching me sends an electrical jolt down my body, centering between my thighs.

"I knew it. Why can't I get enough of you?" His face dives into my neck and his tongue slides up to my ear. His heavy breathing in my ear is like he's strumming my clit. I grow wet from the sound.

"I'm not sure we should be doing this here." My intention with wearing this bikini was so he'd call me later tonight after Emilia falls asleep. I thought we'd flirt a little today—like foreplay—during the barbecue, then we'd seal the deal when there were no witnesses around.

"Fuck it. They're all busy." His hands slide under the back of my bikini bottoms, pushing me into him so his long hard length hits my stomach. Damn, the man is talented, I'll give him that. "Busy with their damn perfect lives."

I still.

He tears off his shirt. The man has abs I could definitely clean my soaked bikini bottoms on. Then he's opening his board shorts, taking my hand and putting it on his dick. "See what you do to me?"

God, how long have I waited for those words to come from his mouth?

I stroke him, and his eyes close briefly. "Damn, that feels good."

The more I'm in this room, looking at Posey's prom pictures and all her girly items from high school, the more off it feels. What happens when I leave this room?

I'm back to being Molly, Nikki's best friend, for the rest of the night.

"Jed?" I say.

His hand slides down the front of my bikini bottoms and his fingers dive between my folds, playing with my clit. "Uh huh?"

"I don't think it's a good idea if we do this here. Maybe I can come by tonight."

His lips are on my skin now as his fingers play with me, making it hard to fight him.

"I don't want a booty call tonight, I want it now," he says in a low voice.

"And that's all this is, right?"

There must be something in my tone I didn't hear because he rears back, and his hands slip from under my bottoms. He stares at me long and hard. "Don't tell me you're gonna make things complicated now?"

There's anger lacing his tone. Anger I've never heard from Jed before.

"Should I just spread my legs when you say go?" I snipe.

Sometimes lately—after Emilia got here—when he looks at me, it's no longer the same Jed. He's lost somewhere, and I have no idea where or how to help him escape the trap he's put himself in.

"I thought we agreed to no strings?"

"We did," I say.

A cocky smile forms on his lips. He approaches me, and for a moment, I allow myself to be his distraction. What's the harm? I don't have feelings for Jed Greene. At least not anything more than lust. Ugh. Even I know I'm lying to myself.

A knock on the door sounds and I push Jed off me, but he must be drunk on lust because he comes right back like I'm playing some game. He grabs my ass and pulls me toward him.

"Jed?" a deep male voice says, and Jed freezes. "Oh shit."

Fisher's eyes pierce into mine when I look around Jed's large body.

"Get the fuck out," Jed says, whipping his head toward his brother.

Fisher's face falls and he shuts the door. Then we hear laughter.

"Oh my God, he won't tell Nikki, will he?" I grab my bikini top off the floor to fasten it back on. "She'll kill me."

"What are you doing? Fisher won't say anything. Keep that off." Jed reaches for my bikini top, but I manage to get dressed and slide away from him.

"I think this was a bad idea."

"So now you're gonna bail on me?" Jed sits on the edge of the bed, his board shorts still open.

I step forward but manage to keep myself far enough away from him. We never should have started whatever this is between us.

"Just go, Molly," he says.

I leave, but mostly to tell Fisher that if he speaks a word of this, I'm coming after him with a meat grinder.

Sneaking down the stairs, I hear Nikki talking from somewhere in the house and guilt weighs heavy on my heart. I'd never want to risk our friendship, but maybe Nikki would be cool with me dating her brother.

I shake my head. What the hell am I thinking? Jed

Greene's been emotionally unavailable my entire life. Nothing's changed. In fact, it's worse.

Ethel

"WE HAVE our work cut out for us, Dori," I say to my best friend on the way home from the Greene family summer bash.

Midge is sleeping in the back seat with her dentures slipping from her mouth. I swear she naps more than a newborn.

"Why's that?" Dori sits in the passenger seat of her Cadillac, which I always drive because the sheriff in Lake Starlight has been on her about driving for years.

"Jed."

"The man who can get a roomful of women to drop their panties?" She chuckles.

"That's the one. The one with the daughter now."

Dori looks out the window. "She's precious."

"I know, but Jed told me he doesn't want to ever be married. His father did a number on him. So now we have to find the true Jed Greene and pull him out."

She laughs. "I'm not sure anyone could manage that man. Now he has a daughter, and as cute as that little girl is, some women might not want to involve themselves in such a situation."

Dori's right. This is a complicated case.

I grip the steering wheel tighter. "That's why I said it's not going to be easy."

"I thought we were working on Allie next anyway. That poor girl needs a man."

I don't bring up my suspicions that Allie and Fisher might be something more than friends. I can't very well set up Allie with Cameron Baker when my own grandson looked murderous when I told him my intentions. We're not there yet. First things first.

"I think we move forward with Jed," I say. "He needs some saving, but only if we can figure out the right girl."

There's a long beat of silence between us.

"What about the sweet librarian?" Dori asks.

"Clara?"

"Yes, Presley's twin."

"They're not twins, Dori. Do you pay attention?" I shake my head.

She huffs. "I'm old. Give me a break."

"Anyone in Lake Starlight for Jed?"

Dori shakes her head.

"We could ask Midge about her grandchildren in Greywall?" I say.

"Yeah, maybe…"

I turn the corner and see a car pulled off on the side of the road. A girl is positioning a jack under the car to replace the tire.

"Isn't that the bar girl?" Dori asks.

I think it's shameful that I know every one of Dori's grandchildren and she can't get mine straight, or their friends who are always hanging around.

"It's Nikki's BFF, Molly." I pull over to the side of the

road and lower the window. "Do you need some help? I could call one of my grandsons?"

Molly laughs. "No, thank you. I can change a tire."

She turns and gets back to work. I watch her to make sure she stays safe, and sure enough, she does it all with no help. An idea comes to mind.

"How would you like to have a drink with Dori and me?" I ask while she's putting the jack away.

Molly looks at me over her shoulder. "Um… sure."

"Great. Follow me to a bar in Lake Starlight, Lucky's."

She nods, and I turn the key and roll up the window.

"What's that about?" Dori asks.

"I may have found the one for Jed, but this will be tricky. We have to do some recon first, because if we're going to try to fix him up with her, we have to know for sure we'll be successful. We won't get a second chance with him."

Dori smiles at me. "I do love a challenge."

I always thank the stars above for bringing Dori into my life. We couldn't be more alike.

"Let's do this, Thelma."

"I'm Louise, you're Thelma," she says.

"No way."

Then we laugh and agree to disagree.

Twenty minutes later, Molly sits across from us in a booth with no idea what she's in for. I love being a grandma.

The End

The Baileys

Lessons from a One-Night Stand (FREE)

Advice from a Jilted Bride

Birth of a Baby Daddy

Operation Bailey Wedding (Novella)

Falling for My Brother's Best Friend

Demise of a Self-Centered Playboy

Confessions of a Naughty Nanny

Operation Bailey Babies (Novella)

Secrets of the World's Worst Matchmaker

Winning my Best Friend's Girl

Rules for Dating Your Ex

Operation Bailey Birthday (Novella)

The Greene Family

My Twist of Fortune (Free Prequel)

My Beautiful Neighbor (FREE)

My Almost Ex

My Vegas Groom

A Greene Family Summer Bash (Novella)

My Sister's Flirty Friend

My Unexpected Surprise

My Famous Frenemy

A Greene Family Vacation (Novella)

My Scorned Best Friend

My Fake Fiancé

My Brother's Forbidden Friend

A Greene Family Christmas (Novella)

Lake Starlight

The Problem with Second Chances

The Issue with Bad Boy Roommates

The Trouble with Runaway Brides

The Drawback of Single Dads

Plain Daisy Ranch

One Last Summer

The One I Left Behind

The One I Stood Beside

The One I Didn't See Coming

Modern Love

Charmed by the Bartender

Hooked by the Boxer

Mad about the Banker

Single Dads Club

Real Deal

Dirty Talker

Sexy Beast

Hollywood Hearts

Mister Mom

Animal Attraction

Domestic Bliss

Bedroom Games

Cold as Ice

On Thin Ice

Break the Ice

Chicago Law

Smitten with the Best Man

Tempted by my Ex-Husband

Seduced by my Ex's Divorce Attorney

Blue Collar Brothers

Flirting with Fire

Crushing on the Cop

Engaged to the EMT

White Collar Brothers

Sexy Filthy Boss

Dirty Flirty Enemy

Wild Steamy Hook-up

The Rooftop Crew

My Bestie's Ex

A Royal Mistake

The Rival Roomies

Our Star-Crossed Kiss

The Do-Over

A Co-Workers Crush

Hockey Hotties

Countdown to a Kiss (Free Prequel)

My Lucky #13 (FREE)

The Trouble with #9

Faking it with #41

Tropical Hat Trick (Novella)

Sneaking around with #34

Second Shot with #76

Offside with #55

Kingsmen Football Stars

False Start (Free Prequel)

You Had Your Chance, Lee Burrows

You Can't Kiss the Nanny, Brady Banks

Over My Brother's Dead Body, Chase Andrews

Chicago Grizzlies

On the Defense (Free Prequel)

Something like Hate

Something like Lust

Something like Love

The Nest

Mr. Heartbreaker

Mr. Broody

Mr. S (Title to be revealed)

Mr. C (Title to be revealed)

Holiday Romances

Single and Ready to Jingle

Claus and Effect

Merry Kissmas

Cockamamie Unicorn Ramblings

We hope you enjoyed seeing a glimpse into the Greenes and found some hidden eggs to what's coming for the Greene family members in the future!

Without our team you wouldn't have any of our books! Seriously, they take on a lot of the work so that we can write!

Danielle Sanchez and the entire Wildfire Marketing Solutions team.

Cassie from Joy Editing for line edits.

Ellie from My Brother's Editor for line edits.

My Brother's Editor for proofreading.

Hang Le for the cover and branding for the entire series.

Bloggers who consistently carve out time to read, review and/or promote us.

Piper Rayne Unicorns who love our characters like as much as we do!

Readers who took the time to read our story when there's so many choices out there.

Jed is next Unicorns! We cannot wait for you to get your hands on him!

xo,

Piper & Rayne

About Piper & Rayne

Piper Rayne is a USA Today Bestselling Author duo who write "heartwarming humor with a side of sizzle" about families, whether that be blood or found. They both have e-readers full of one-clickable books, they're married to husbands who drive them to drink, and they're both chauffeurs to their kids. Most of all, they love hot heroes and quirky heroines who make them laugh, and they hope you do, too!

www.ingramcontent.com/pod-product-compliance
Lightning Source LLC
Chambersburg PA
CBHW061550310726
48972CB00008B/2700